Thanks to You

Wisdom from Mother & Child

Photographs from the authors' extended family collection

Julie Andrews Edwards &
Emma Walton Hamilton

HarperCollins*Publishers*

FOREWORD

Writing this book was something of an awakening for us both.

Lessons from parents and grandparents are often handed down and shared with children and grandchildren. But what emerged as we began to write this together was an awareness of how much we've learned from our children—of how motherhood itself has been perhaps the greatest education of our lives. We realized that nothing has taught us more about risk taking, faith, courage, perspective, strength, generosity, the passage of time, or the power of love than being a parent.

We drew on our own experiences to inspire each statement of gratitude in the book. Our hope was that by sharing personal lessons learned, we might also in some way touch the universal. For this same reason, we chose to use photographs from our extended family collection, selecting ones that we thought might reflect a common experience.

A cloud becomes a castle for a king . . . I notice wonder in the smallest thing: We have a family tradition of shared walks in nature—noticing colors, details, smells, sounds; making discoveries. We ask our children to look up, to expand their awareness—but they invite us to share their wonder in the details.

I know that all I have to do is try . . . I understand that it's all right to cry: Whether it's a new food, activity, or challenge, we were always encouraged to "give it a shot" before dismissing it. These days we've learned the importance of acknowledging feelings that might arise in the process.

I'm not afraid to go the extra length . . . I find I have a deeper well of strength: Starting school, traveling alone, a hospital visit—these small acts of courage for us as children now provide us with the necessary perspective to try to be brave and loving parents.

Our mothers have shaped us, but our children define us. It is thanks to them that our

mother-daughter relationship continues to be so gratifying. Was it a coincidence that we finished the first draft of *Thanks to You* on Mother's Day 2006?

We couldn't have given each other a lovelier gift.

—JULIE ANDREWS EDWARDS &
EMMA WALTON HAMILTON
JUNE 2006

Thanks to you...

I spread my wings
and try to touch the sky

Thanks to you...

I trust the leap of faith it takes to fly

Thanks to you...

a cloud becomes
a castle for a king

Thanks to you...

I notice wonder in the smallest thing

Thanks to you...

I recognize
the majesty of trees

Thanks to you...

the more I grow, the more I climb with ease

Thanks to you...

a rainy day
extends an invitation

Thanks to you...

a rainbow is a lovely affirmation

Thanks to you...

I know that all I have to do is try

Thanks to you...

I understand that it's all right to cry

Thanks to you...

I'll be a clown
whenever there's a chance

Thanks to you...

The sound of laughter makes my spirit dance

Thanks to you...

I'm grateful for
the glory of each day

Thanks to you...

there's beauty in the simplest bouquet

Thanks to you...

I like to spend some
quiet time alone

Thanks to you...

I see the fruit of seeds that I have sown

Thanks to you...

I'm not afraid
to go the extra length

Thanks to you...

I find I have a deeper well of strength

Thanks to you...

A day can promise
endless hours of pleasure

Thanks to you...

A moment is a gift I've learned to treasure

Thanks to you…

I take big steps
to conquer a new land

Thanks to you…

I find my purpose in your trusting hand

Thanks to you...

"Home" is more a feeling
than a place

Thanks to you...

I've seen firsthand the miracle of grace

Wherever we may roam,
the same stars will shine above

We're bound by all that's beautiful...

and
by love.

Special thanks to the family members
who helped make this book possible, as well as
Catherine Ashmore; the Damiecki family; the Evans family;
Jen Gosney; Diego Purcell; Anne Runolfsson and Tess Adams; the Smith family;
and, most especially, Zoë Dominic and Francine Taylor.

Acknowledgments photo by Jayne Wexler

Library of Congress Cataloging-in-Publication Data
Edwards, Julie, date
Thanks to you : wisdom from mother & child / Julie Andrews Edwards and Emma Walton Hamilton. — 1st ed.
p.   cm.
Summary: Photographs and verse celebrate the life lessons that mothers and children learn from one another.
ISBN-10: 0-06-124002-8 (trade bdg. : alk. paper) — ISBN-13: 978-0-06-124002-7 (trade bdg. : alk. paper)
[1. Mother and child—Fiction. 2. Gratitude—Fiction. 3. Stories in rhyme.] I. Hamilton, Emma Walton. II. Title.
PZ8.3.E27Tha 2007   2006021718
[E]—dc22   CIP
                                                                                                                                  AC

2 3 4 5 6 7 8 9 10
❖
First Edition